A
Cat's Journey

Finding Joy

By **Marietta Litton**

Illustrations By Cheryl Litton

A Cat's Journey Finding Joy

ISBN: 978-1-087-95149-2

First Edition: 2021

Front Cover image and interior drawings by Cheryl Litton
Book design by Cheryl Litton
More at Hanalu.com

Edited by everyone

Juvenile Literature

Printed in the United States of America, Ingram Sparks

Dedication

To my daughter, Kim, whose love of all animals (the tame, the wild, the unloved, and the abandoned) inspired this story.

Preface

Most stories begin with "Once upon a time…", but my story begins with, "There was a time once…"

There was a time once that I had Mother, brothers and sisters. There was a time once that I lived my life, as a cat, with a few friends in a big noisy congested city. There was a time once when I was never held in someone's arms and was told, "I love you" or had a name of my very own. Most of all there was a time once that I had four sturdy legs.

I want to share my story with you about my life walking around on those four legs but with very little joy, and how my life changed. By some shocking and amazing sequence of events, I found myself with only three legs but with much joy, a special name of my very own, and in arms that loved me.

How did these things become possible? How could life on four legs become so much better on only three? Who would think that a tragedy one afternoon would turn into such wonderful new beginnings? This is my story of how I searched for joy, and how joy found me.

Contents

1. First Memories 1

2. New Adventures 9

3. A Home with Loud Mouth 21

4. Meeting Cornelius 31

5. Making Friends with a Mouse 43

6. Discovering New Friends 54

7. The Terrible Accident 65

8. A Life at the Clinic 76

9. Wonderments Coming True 85

1

There was a time once of ...

First Memories

First memories have always been the best place to start when one is sharing their life's story, so I have begun my story with my earliest recollections. My first weeks of life were pleasant times of feeling warmed and snuggled. My only problem was that I could hear, but I could not see anything. I lived in total darkness. No matter how hard I tried to open my eyes, they felt glued shut and would not budge. I knew that there were others around me because I felt wet noses brushing past my face. Wobbly bodies kept bumping against me. The bodies had strange weak sounds coming from them. I made the same weak sounds too, but we didn't understand what we were saying or trying to say.

Our mother was very attentive. I have memories of her licking my face and body. Her tongue was both rough and smooth at the same time, and I didn't mind. There were mealtimes and being very close to Mother. That was when I was warmed, loved, and the most content. Of course sometimes one of the "wobblers", who was stumbling around in the dark just like me, ended up pushing me away from Mother. She would just gently nudge me back to her. For weeks that's how things went. I moved around in the dark bumping into and whining with those nearest me. Most of the time was spent, getting as close as possible to Mother, drinking warm milk, and then dozing off to sleep.

One day an amazing thing happened! I woke up as usual from my soft, warm place, but this time, it was because noise and excitement were coming from the moving bodies right next to me. I tried to open my eyes, and to my astonishment they popped open! At first I saw only light mixed with dark shadows. After a few minutes, things became much clearer and in focus. The excitement and noises were the voices of my brothers and sisters. I could understand them perfectly! The same words were being repeated over and over again, and voices were overlapping each other saying, "Mother, is that you?"

Then I heard her voice. She said, "Yes, my Precious Kittens." From that day on she called us "Kittens". When she spoke to only one of us at a time, she would call each of us, "Precious".

A Cat's Journey Finding Joy

As she instructed, we called each other only "Brother" or "Sister". That first day of sight, we walked around all day saying, "Hello, Brother" and "Hello, Sister." I was one of the Brothers!

I had brothers and sisters with a variety of colors and distinct markings. There were shades of grays and browns along with blacks and whites running everywhere. As for myself, my shades of browns were mixed with golden tones. The darkest browns were stripes that ran north and south from my back to my stomach and east to west across my chest and legs. Mother said things to us such as; there's my little snowball or my little brown bear. For me, Mother said that I was her little tiger. Of course, it wasn't until much later that we understood the things she said about us. Mostly that first day, we snuggled next to Mother because it was so good to finally see her.

Our home was in a corner of a room called a garage. We saw that our place was a very large

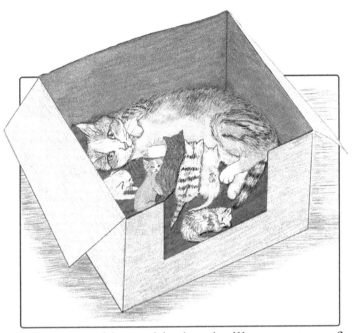

box with a big multicolored pillow on top of which Mother and all of us lay. The sides of the box were much taller than Mother except for one side that had an opening that was removed a few inches up from the floor.

Many days we were allowed to walk out of the box and look around. Mother watched us and let us explore. We were full of questions and kept asking, "What's that?" "What's this?" Mother answered all of our questions. She would say, "That's a bike." "That's a rake." "That's a bucket." She often said with love, "Stay where I can see you!" We always did what Mother said.

One day we were exploring, as Mother watched, and two strange tall beings came towards us. We all started running to Mother crying hysterically, and she gathered us close. The strange beings bent down and very gently rubbed Mother's head and around her ears. Mother wasn't afraid and made a soft wonderful sound. They told Mother how beautiful her "Kittens" were. They picked up a few brothers and sisters to rub their heads too. We learned that the strange two-legged beings were our mother's family. That meant that she belonged to them as we did also. They set out something in a small bowl and placed each of us near it. We looked in and smelled something very appetizing. One brother took a bite and then another and said, "Wow, this stuff is good." All of us tried it and agreed. We ate until our bellies grew to twice their sizes and were bulging out on both sides of our bodies. The two beings watched and laughed for quite a while. As they left, I heard one say to Mother, "Good Night, Lilly."

Later we asked Mother what "Lilly" meant, and she told us that it was the name given to her by her two-legged family. Their names were Lucy and William. She was given to them, as a kitten herself, a few years ago. Lucy is the one who named her, Lilly, because she thought Mother was as pretty as a flower.

We all wanted a name too! We asked Mother to please give us a name. Mother told us that we would just be called her "Precious Kittens" for now. She told us that in a few weeks each of us would be leaving her and going to our new two-legged families. Then we would be given our very own names. Each of us said, "No, Mother!" " We never want to leave you ever!"

Mother explained that Lucy and William were her family. They loved her very much, and she loved them. She soothed us to sleep that night. She told us that we would have wonderful loving families. We would receive wonderful names too. She assured us, for a cat, that's the way it is. We are born to bring love and companionship, and in return we will be loved and cared for too. She said that sorrow will come with each parting, but it would soon be replaced with great joy. This she promised each of us.

"Sometimes you will never know the value of a moment until it becomes a memory."

Dr. Seuss
Author and Illustrator

2

There was a time once of ...

New Adventures

One day after breakfast, Mother said she was going somewhere. We were to stay near the box. My Best Brother who was gray in color came up to me when Mother left. I called him my "Best Brother" because he and I played together the most. We enjoyed wrestling and rolling around on the floor all the time. My sisters were not

interested in that kind of play, and my other brothers wanted to nap all day.

He said, "Do you want to go exploring?"

I timidly replied, "No, Mother told us to stay right here near the box."

"We won't go far. I promise," he said as he looked to the areas beyond the box.

10

"Just think about all the things out there that we haven't discovered yet!"

"I'm scared, and I'm not sure we should go," I said looking out in the direction of his eyes and then back at the box. There was something in my heart or somewhere within me that kept telling me that disobeying Mother was a bad idea.

"Then I'm going without you," he said over his shoulder as he walked forward.

I was so worried that he would get lost that I followed behind him for a short distance.

"What if I stood closer to the box, and you look around? You can keep calling out to me, and when I call back, you will know how to return."

"That sounds like a plan to me!" he said as he took off running.

He was so excited that he started going to his left, then to his right, and then back to his left again.

He called out "Wow!" "What's that?" "What's this?"

I shouted back, "What does it look like?"

All of a sudden, he came running back towards me and said, "You've gotta see this!"

"What is it?" I was now as excited as he was.

"It's a big black mountain!" he said running out of sight again.

I was so excited that, without thinking, I ran after him. As I turned the corner, there it was right on the floor in front of me. It was a humongous black mountain! It was so high that we had to hold our heads all the way back to even see the top. Its steep sides were cliff-like and were lined with different horizontal layers. The layers formed a pattern with some layers protruding out further than others.

"Let's climb the mountain and explore!" Brother shouted.

With my mouth hanging open and eyes staring up at the steep cliff of the mountain, I managed to say, "How do we do that?"

Brother stared at the mountain for a moment and said, "Watch this!" He pushed out his claws and caught a hold of one of the protruding layers. Slowly he went up with his right front paw, left front paw, and back paws following. Soon he was at the very top of the mountain. No sooner had he gotten to the top, he mysteriously disappeared. He let out a yell, and then all went silent.

I yelled out to him, but he did not answer. I was not only terrified but also extremely worried for my brother. With my eyes shut, I started to climb the mountain just the way Best Brother had done. I went up slowly with right front paw, left front paw, and with back paws following. I made my way to the top. There was a gigantic hole in the middle of the mountain! Looking down, I saw Best Brother unharmed and looking around. I looked down at him and shouted angrily, "You scared me to death! Why didn't you answer me and let me know that you were OK?"

All he would say repeatedly while ignoring my anger was, "You are **not** going to believe this! I mean you are really not going to believe this!"

"What?" "What?" I said, now really getting annoyed. It surprised me how quickly my fear and worry had changed into anger.

"I was falling, and I landed on my feet! I actually landed on all **four** of my paws without even trying. Isn't that amazing? Now, you try because there is something you really need to see down here."

Anger was being replaced with curiosity! I couldn't explain why I had listened to Best Brother in the first place. In my heart I knew I shouldn't have, and now here I was ready again to do whatever he said. First, I wanted to see if I would land on all four paws just like him. Second, I wanted to see what he was seeing. I shut my eyes again and jumped. I nearly landed right on top of Best Brother!

He started to laugh and said, "See, what did I tell you?"

"Wow" was all I could say over and over again because, just as he had said, I landed on all four paws automatically without even trying.

"Now look in here. It's like a cave!"

At that he jumped inside a cave-like indented area. It was dark and inside the mountain, but it was not scary because we were still near the lighted open area where we landed in the center. I stepped up slightly and entered the cave. Best Brother then started to run, and I ran after him. It appeared that we were running around and around in circles, but that's what made it so much fun. We played hard and long. I chased him, and then he chased me. We ran until we both fell over dizzy and exhausted.

He said, "Brother, that was fun!" I agreed.

We didn't intend to, but we both fell asleep. It was hunger that caused me to awake first. I moved over to Best Brother and nudged him awake.

"I'm getting hungry, and we have been gone a long time because we fell asleep. Let's get back before Mother knows we are gone." My words made me feel awful immediately because they were about deceiving Mother. I corrected my self quickly by saying, "I mean we need to get back before Mother sees us gone and gets worried." Still the changing of my words did not help me to feel any better.

He yawned and said, "OK". I looked over at him and his eyes widened.

"What?" I said

"How are we going to get back up to the top of the mountain?" This was said with a trembling voice that I had never heard from him before.

We both looked up to the top of the mountain. It looked so much higher than before. On this side of the mountain there was no cliff to climb. There was only the open cave area that we had played so hard and long in. My brave exploring Best Brother did not appear so brave now. He was as fearful as me and was the first to cry.

"Don't cry," I told him as calm as I could. "We are not too far from home. Mother will find us."

"But how?" he sniffled taking his paw to rub over his eyes.

"Let's take turns calling her," I said trying to control my shaking voice. So that's what we did until both our throats were dry and hurting.

About the time that I was going to cry too, I heard Mother!

"Precious!" " Precious!"

"Over here. Over the mountain and near

the cave!" We both yelled at the same time with voices that trembled.

I am not sure how it happened, but immediately Mother appeared! She was licking us and fussing at us at the same time. Suddenly, she grabbed Best Brother by the back of his neck and carried him off. I knew by the look in her eyes that I had better stay put until she returned for me. Of course, I had nowhere else to go. Soon she was back, and I was lifted up and over the top of the mountain and onto the big safe pillow. Brothers and Sisters were so glad to see us because they had been so worried about us. I felt bad that I had disobeyed Mother and caused her to worry. Mother told us that we were not to ever go out and about without her again.

The look of love and pain in Mother's eyes that day taught me an important lesson. I learned to always listen to her.

The world beyond our box was a very big place and was full of mysterious objects. I was too young to know about the things of the world that could really hurt me, and I had much to learn first before going out on my own. I also learned to listen to my heart. If it doesn't feel right about doing something, it's best not to do it, even if it's with your own "Best Brother". I learned to be careful and not to get into situations that I couldn't get out of on my own. Oh, by the way, Mother told us that our mountain wasn't a mountain after all, but it was an object called a tire.

I stayed close to Mother, Brothers, and Sisters after that, until the days came for Goodbyes.

"Youth is the spirit of adventure and awakening..."

Ezra Taft Benson
Farmer, government official (1953-61),
religious leader

3

There was a time once of …

A Home with Loud Mouth

The days came for our goodbyes, and they came one after another. There were moments of sorrow like Mother mentioned, but she reminded each of us again that we would have our own families, our own names, and great joys. As my Best Brother left, I felt that the sorrow was too great, and there could be no amount of joy that would replace it.

My turn to leave Mother came one Friday morning. Before I was to be placed in a small box by Lucy, she let Mother say goodbye to me. Mother licked the top of my head, as I snuggled close to her for one last time. She told me not to be sad. She reminded me that my sorrow would soon be replaced with fun and happiness with my new family. Her sorrow would be replaced with the thoughts of the families loving each of her "Precious Kittens". I kept my eyes locked on Mother's eyes until I was lifted up and placed into that small box.

The box and I were placed on the backseat of a car. Lucy was in the front seat with William, and she kept leaning back to rub my head and to assure me that I would be OK. I could see what Mother had meant about receiving love and joy from these affectionate beings.

After what seemed like a very long time, the car stopped. As I was taken out of the car, I noticed the sounds of my new surroundings. It had been so quiet in our home with only the sounds of my brothers and sisters and the low hum of the dryer in the corner of the garage. Now there were horns honking constantly and the swishing sounds of fast moving objects on the street. In the distance there was the sound of a siren and the whistle of a train. There were voices of people that were coming from the sidewalks and stairways to houses that were connected side by side. We went up one of the stairways, and William knocked on a door. I couldn't see out, but I found myself getting excited because soon I would meet my family and get my very own name. Of course, I would receive the great joy that Mother was always speaking about too.

A Cat's Journey Finding Joy

After a second knock on the door and an even longer wait, it finally opened. A loud voice said, "Oh, it's here. Just set the box over there." I about jumped out of the box at the sound of that voice. It was louder than the time we knocked over the rake in the garage and ran to Mother afraid for our lives. It was louder than the first time we heard thunder on that stormy Sunday afternoon. Lucy quickly placed her hand in the box and on top of my head to help soothe me. Why couldn't the voice be as quiet as the voices of Lucy and William? William started to tell the loud voice what a wonderful cat I was, and the loud voice only said, "That's good. I only hope it knows how to catch a mouse!"

As Lucy placed the box on the floor she said, "Here's your new home, darling," and then they were gone.

Without a sound, a bowl of food and water

were placed in the box with me. I fell asleep thinking my name and joy would come tomorrow.

Days and weeks went by, but there was no family, no joy, and no name of my own, only Loud Mouth (which was the name I decided to give my owner). I didn't receive a name, but I had a whole group of names given to me. Sometimes I was called Cat, or Mouser, or just Nuisance. Sometimes I was even called, Good for Nothing. I outgrew my box and was allowed to move about the house. I soon learned not to go near Loud Mouth. I was thankful that she always wore large pink soft slippers because sometimes she would use her foot to forcedly push me away. All I wanted was to affectionately rub up against her like I saw Mother do many times with her family. Mother always received a loving pat or was picked up with arms for a sweet

hug whenever she did that. I also found out the hard way not to even think about wanting to curl up on her lap! She did give me a rug to lie on in the kitchen. I was given food and water but no love.

Each morning, I was sent out for the day through the door she held open and each night the loud voice let me back in. During the day, I just walked around and took naps in the alley until dark. The door was always opened for me at night even though sometimes I was uncertain if it would be. One night, I even lay on the steps until morning. Loud Mouth reminded me often that there was only one reason that I had a home with her. That reason was to catch mice! The loud voice would say that I had better do my job or else. That was not family. That was not joy, and I felt only sorrow still. I thought of my Mother often and my brothers and sisters.

Were they happy? Did they have a family of their own, their own name, and great joy? I hoped that their lives were better than mine.

Day after day the same thing happened. Loud Mouth would wake up and sometimes she would scream about "that mouse". On those days she would practically throw me out the door saying, "You, Good for Nothing! You are here to get that mouse, and you had better get him!"

A mouse, a mouse, I was so tired of hearing about that mouse. I guess I must be the soundest sleeper of all cats in the world or maybe the whole universe because I never heard that mouse, not even once. I figured he must have been wearing pink slippers just like Loud Mouth. He came sure enough because even I could see the crumbs left, and some were even inches away from me. Once I thought that it looked like some of my own food was missing! It was her threats that bothered me the most. They were threats about not letting me back in ever, if I didn't do my job.

After a morning of screaming and being pushed out the door, I found myself leaving with my head hanging down even lower than usual. I started to think that maybe I was a "Good for Nothing". Mother only spoke about joys not jobs to do. I was glad she did not see the situation I was in because I know she would have had as much sorrow as I was having now.

My mind was cluttered with the thoughts, as I did my morning routines. I walked down the steps as usual onto the sidewalk. I walked past the other steps as usual on my way to the alley, but this time something unusual happened. Someone called out to me, "Hey you, Young One, come here a minute."

"Sadness is but a wall between two gardens."

Khalid Gibran
Lebanese artist, poet, and writer

4

There was a time once of...

Meeting Cornelius

I looked around to see who spoke but mostly to see if they were speaking to me. "Over here on the steps in front of you. I would like to speak with you."

like to speak with you."

I looked up and at the top of the steps lay a rather large black mass. What struck me most was his enormous size and amount of hair. I had

not seen another cat with so much hair and so much longer in length than my own, and he was twice the size of my mother. I would have been afraid of such size and mass if it hadn't been for his brilliant blue eyes. They were eyes like I had not seen before either. It was not their color that was so different, but the way they commanded you with authority and kindness at the same time. I knew that Loud Mouth had authority over my existence, and she used her mouth to make known her demands. The enormous cat's eyes showed authority and were making a demand without even saying a word. I knew he had something to say to me, and I needed to listen to him. I didn't feel threatened because those same eyes looked concerned and even appeared to care about me!

He said, "I'm Cornelius. I've been watching you each day, and today it looks like the perfect day for us to converse. Come and have a seat."

I came closer and looking into those eyes, I decided I best do what he requested. I sat beside him, and he made no move to sit up, but kept reclining as I first found him.

"Young One, by what name are you called?"

"Why Sir, I am called many names. One is Cat, one is Mouser, one is Nuisance, and one is Good for Nothing," I replied wondering what reaction I would receive.

He sat staring at me for a moment and then said, "Well, Well." After another minute he said, "Well, for starters Cat is not a name. It is what you are. Mouser is not a name. It's what you do. You know like a singer's job is to sing, a runner's job is to run, a sailor's job is to sail, so a mouser's job is to get a mouse. Nuisance and Good for Nothing are not names because they are matters of opinion. So I agreed that you are a cat. Are you a mouser?"

"Sir, at this time I am not a mouser because I have not caught a mouse yet or have even seen one."

"Well, are you of the opinion that you are a Nuisance or Good for Nothing?"

"Sir, I don't think that I cause much of a problem, but sometimes I meow for food when my dish is empty, or when I have no water. That's when I'm the most of a nuisance it seems. As for being, Good for Nothing, I guess that's because I haven't caught any mice yet. I think that's the only reason that I exist in my home."

"Well, that explains everything," he said as he stretched out almost the length of the porch.

"Explains what, Sir?"

"Your sorrow and sadness. Every morning I sit here and see you walking by with your head down. I bet this is the only time you have ever seen me here. Am I right?

I also bet that you would not have seen me today either, if I had not called out to you. I am willing to also suggest that you have never seen, Officer Chris, sitting on his steps each morning reading his paper before going to work. He watches you each day, and you never even look up."

All I could think about were his first words, and I asked him with a quivering voice, "Sir, you see my sorrow? My Mother told us that we would have sorrow at our partings, but it would be replaced with a new family, a name of our very own, and great joy. I don't have the family I thought I would, I don't have a real name of my own, and I have no joy."

"Well, well," he said again and was silent for a very long time.

At last he spoke. "Young One, but first, is it OK if I add this name to your collection of names?" I nodded my head because it was like

36

being called Cat, but coming from him it had an affectionate sound.

He continued, "You see sometimes we expect joy, and it's not there. We have to look for it and find it in the things around us right where we are. If you would try to find some simple joys right where you are now, you may be a little happier with your situation, until the joy your mother spoke of finds you. You can't go on in such sorrow that you miss out on the nicer things around you like meeting me." At this there was a glint of mischief in his eyes, and for the first time I smiled. I realized that I had held my head down for so long I had missed the opportunity to see and speak to this wise old cat.

"Sir, how do I find the joy around me until joy finds me?"

"First, you have to think of the good

and not the bad all the time. You have shelter, food, and water. Maybe the joy you seek in your home is not there because of the lack of love, but you have freedom all day to find joy in moments. Now, face the Sun. Do you feel that warmth?"

I raised my face upwards towards the Sun and had to admit it did feel good.

"Now, that's a moment of joy. Isn't it? There's nothing better than to stretch out and let that Sun just shine on you. It's a lot better than napping in a dark damp alley. Now close your eyes and listen. Do you hear the songs of the birds?" He paused for a moment and said; "Now some cats like to attack birds, but not me because that would silence such sweet melodies."

I did as he said and listened closely. I could hear a robin singing high up among the tree branches. There were other sounds coming from a few trees down of another bird, but that bird had a deeper tone. He was adding perfectly to the song of the first. In that moment I found a bit of joy!

Cornelius broke my trance to say something really important. "Young One, I want you to start today seeing, hearing, and feeling the joys around you. You have missed much in your sorrow. How can joy find you when you walk around with your head down and in such misery?"

I promised him that I would try to work on my appearances of sadness, but I still had a problem. Something told me that this wise old cat could help.

"As you know one of my names is Mouser. Loud Mouth says that if I don't do my job I am out of there! I will find myself without a home. What would be the joy in that?"

"Loud Mouth!" " Well, Young One, I see you have named someone most perfectly. If I didn't know where you lived, I know now because I know exactly of whom you are speaking. I never understood why some people speak such. Maybe she was a teacher once. Anyway, back to your problem. Is there a mouse in your house?"

"I think so because Loud Mouth screams some mornings that it has been there, but I have not heard or seen it. I have seen a few crumbs here and there. He must be the cleverest and quietest mouse in the city because he goes about the kitchen and even right next to where I sleep. Anyway, I wouldn't know what to do with a mouse, even if I saw one much less caught one."

"Then I suggest you stay up all night and find the joy of making friends with a mouse,"

40

Cornelius said as if cats should be friends with mice. I knew that I wouldn't mind catching a mouse, but then what? I surely never wanted to actually eat one. Did Cornelius know this about me from our first meeting?

"Well Sir, you have given me a lot to think about. Can I come again to talk?"

"Of course you can, now that you will be looking up, right? Come anytime you see me even if it appears that I'm sleeping. I won't mind at all bringing a moment of joy to you in giving you a chance to speak with me." Again there was that twinkle of mischievousness in his eyes.

I left his porch and started home, but this time I lifted my face and felt the warmth of the sun. I walked past steps and noticed people, and one even spoke to me. I saw mothers pushing their babies in strollers, and I heard excited words from small voices saying "Kitty, Kitty." I went up the steps to my home and lay down until the door was opened for me. As I went past Loud Mouth, she said, "Get in, Nuisance!"

I went to my food dish, ate, and sank down onto my rug. I said to myself, "Tonight I will stay awake and wait for that mouse. But what did Cornelius say? Make friends with a mouse!"

"When we are no longer able to change a situation, we are challenged to change ourselves."

Viktor Frankl
Australian neurologist, psychiatrist, and Holocaust survivor

5

There was a time once of…

Making Friends with a Mouse

That night, as I forced myself to stay awake, I heard the faint noise of scurrying feet. I thought that I saw a gray blur run around the corner. I got to my feet and crept slowly and saw a skinny hairless tail sticking out from behind the stove. Was this a mouse? I had not actually seen one. It must be the mouse Loud Mouth

43

has been screaming about. Lightening fast and in one pounce, I surprisingly found that I held onto the hairless tail. A weird squeal came from behind the stove, and then a panic-stricken voice said, "Please, please, don't eat me!"

I drew my paw forward to see what strange creature was making such a shrill sound. Before my eyes, I saw a small fat body with four short stubby legs and small round ears.

"Why would I eat you?" I asked.

"Why isn't that what cats are suppose to do?" answered the chubby mouse.

"What are you?" I inquired wanting to be sure I wasn't talking to some other kind of rodent.

"Why, I'm a mouse!" As he said this, he stood up on his hind legs to look at me, and it appeared that the question had shocked him. Then he began to talk so fast that I was not sure that I could keep up. "I've been around here a very long time. Usually you are sleeping so soundly that I can do just about anything I want to. Tonight you were awake and surprised me, which was very careless on my part. Were you waiting for me? I know what cats do. Just go ahead and do it but be quick!" At this he got back down on all four legs and tucked his head between his front feet.

"What if I don't want to eat you?" I was hoping the mouse would give me some other suggestions. His head rose up to look at me. I saw in his very small round eyes that fear was leaving and was replaced with a look of relief.

"Well I'd be very happy to hear that you wouldn't want to eat me, but then we will have a problem. How are we going to handle it? I've heard what Pink Feet calls you. She calls you, Mouser."

"Wait, who is…"I stopped when I realized that he called Loud Mouth, "Pink Feet".

"Never mind, please continue." I said.

"Well, if you are a Mouser and I'm a

mouse, then you are the one who is supposed to take care of me. You know like a gardener takes care of a garden, a singer takes care of the song, and an eater takes care of eating. Get it? For a mouser to take care of a mouse usually means to get rid of it!"

"Yes, I've heard this before, but I have no plans to eat you tonight or ever."

"That's the problem that we need to solve," he said as he began to pace back and forth on his hind legs and with no apparent fear. He placed his tiny front foot-paw to his head, as if he could grab a solution right out of it. He paused for a moment just like Cornelius and then said, "For you to keep your home, you have to do your job. At least that's what I've heard Pink Feet say. I have a plan that will help both of us."

"What's the plan?"

"You let me have pieces of your food, and I will help you to do your job about once a week."

"Go on."

"We will wait until Pink Feet wakes up. I'll run across the floor, and I'll let you catch me."

"You will **let me** catch you?"

"When **you** catch me, take me in your mouth and carry me…"

"WAIT! Take you into my MOUTH!" I screamed so loud it made the mouse jump twice his height.

"Yes, just for a little while until you get outside, and then I can jump out. That way I continue to get some food for my family, and you get to keep your home."

It could work I thought, but the thought of a mouse in my mouth for the distance and time needed almost made me sick. Then I thought about the "what ifs". What if Loud Mouth Pink Feet (Mouse and I decided to combine the names into one) did throw me out on the street not to let me return? Where was I to go? At the moment I had no great joy, but definitely there would be no joy at all in having no home. How could joy ever find me, if I was looking for shelter and food? No, I had to go along with his plan and find the joy in it until a better plan came along.

I finally made a decision and said, "It's a deal!"

"Then for this to work we must practice!" he said.

"Practice?"

"Yes, it has to be believable. Open your mouth. I'll get in and for a good effect I will leave my tail hanging out."

With disgust, I opened my mouth and mouse crawled in. He curled up into a ball and lay on my tongue. Since he was a rather chubby mouse, I felt my jaws puffing out on each side. The first practice grossed both of us out. I had mouse hair in my mouth, and he had cat slobber all over.

We practiced a few more times. Mouse learned how to lie in my mouth without causing me to choke, and I learned not to slobber so much. His tail hanging out of my mouth did make for a good effect. We stayed up all night talking and practicing. Mouse carried a few pieces of my food home and returned before morning, so that we could perform our plan.

49

When he arrived right before dawn, I asked Mouse, "Why are you doing this for me? You have been taking food for a long time, and I have not even heard you. You could continue to do so without this plan. I mean you trust me not to hurt you. I am even slobbering all over you!"

"Well, I'm getting older, and it's more dangerous for me to climb around like I use to. You are sharing your food, which I must add is rather tasty, without me doing all the work. Plus, you look like you could use a friend to help you keep your home, such as it is."

Yes, he was right. That was my home, and there was a moment of joy in knowing that having a home was a good thing!

Mouse and I decided to take a little nap because we were so exhausted from practicing all night. We were startled awake when Loud Mouth Pink Feet came into the kitchen to make her coffee. As usual she walked past me without a word. Exactly as planned, Mouse ran across the floor. Loud Mouth Pink Feet saw him and started shouting.

"Get it!" "Get it!"

I went into action chasing mouse left, right, and left again. We went under the table and around the stove. Once we even ran across Loud Mouth Pink Feet's feet! Finally out of her sight, I opened my mouth and let mouse jump in. I must say the best part was when I faced Loud Mouth Pink Feet with Mouse in my mouth. My cheeks were all puffed out, and his skinny hairless tail was swaying back and forth between my lips. Loud Voice Pink Feet let out a scream that could be heard two doors down, into the street, and at least a block away!

"Take that thing outside now!", she yelled as she stomped to the door and opened it wide.

She kept pointing and shouting over and over.

"Get it out!" "Get it out!"

51

A Cat's Journey Finding Joy

I went out, down the steps to the sidewalk, and made my way to the alley. Cornelius was on his porch and propped up as I carried my head high and proudly with Mouse's tail swaying back and forth from my lips.

"Looks like you are finding a little joy today! Come later and tell me all about it!"

I turned my eyes to Cornelius. I was afraid to smile and lose Mouse right there on the sidewalk. Once in the alley, I opened my mouth and let Mouse jump out. We laughed and laughed, as I spit hair from my mouth, and he wiped away slobber from his fur. We both understood right there and then what was meant when someone said that they almost died from laughing.

Cornelius was right! I needed to make friends with a mouse and I did! We did our routine at least 2-3 times a month. Mouse would come a few times a week for his reward of food. I really enjoyed his visits, but he could never stay long. I remembered what Cornelius said. He said to find the joy in each moment, and my moments with Mouse were joy. He was my friend by night, and soon I would find even more friends by day!

"Always turn a negative situation into a positive situation."

Michael Jordan

Former professional basketball player

6

There was a time once of…

Discovering New Friends

Since meeting Mouse and Cornelius, my life started to have some simple joys. Each day I would walk up to Officer Chris, as he read the paper, for my daily rub. I stopped to talk with Cornelius, and then I strolled along the sidewalk.

One day as I was walking, I heard some shouts coming from across the street.

"Hey, do you want to come over here?" I looked across the street and was surprised to see three cats about my age. I looked around to be sure that they were taking to me when one called out again.

"Hey, come on over. We have been watching you for a while and thought maybe you would like to hang out with us on our side of the street."

"I would like that, but I have never crossed a street before," I shouted back excited and nervous at the same time.

A shorthaired gray cat that reminded me of Best Brother shouted, "Well, you have to look left, then right, then left again, and then run like a wild cat with its tail on fire." At that all three started to laugh, as if it was the funniest thing ever said. Maybe they had actually seen a wild cat with its tail on fire!

There was something about the three laughing cats that made me want to get to know them better. I never liked going near the street. The thought of crossing it made my legs feel too weak to even hold my body up. Before I could talk myself out of the idea, I found my mouth shouting back to them, "Here I come!" I looked left, then right, and then left again. When there weren't any fast moving objects coming, I ran as fast as a wild cat with its tail on fire. When I got to the other side, my heart was beating so fast I thought I'd pass out. Before I could catch my breath and get the strength back to my legs, they all shouted, "Come on." They took off, and I followed. They finally stopped, and without panting like I was, introduced themselves. The gray one said, "I'm called Gray. Do you get it?" Again they all laughed like he had said a very funny statement, but there was something about their laughter that made me automatically laugh too. These cats definitely knew "joy".

The white cat with scattered black spots said, "I'm Dots."

The third one was the smallest. He was solid black except for a white area around his mouth that made him look like he was smiling all the time.

"My name is Luca," he said with such pride. He stretched his head high, and in that moment, he appeared taller and bigger than all of us.

"So what's your name?" Gray said.

All eyes were on me as I tried to think of what to tell them. I could tell that they had families that cared about them. They had real names that matched them perfectly, and they did seem so full of joy. They were happy cats with happy families, and I could tell it immediately.

"Well," I stammered, "I am a cat with many names. I have a different name for each day of the week."

"Wow", said Luca. "I never met an animal with more than one name before."

"Some days I'm called Mouser, some

days I'm called Nuisance, and some days I'm called Good." I couldn't tell them that the name was actually, Good for Nothing. I went on to tell them about my friend Cornelius who called me, Young One, and Officer Chris who called me, Fella.

"Wow" was all they could say.

After a little silence, Dots looked at the others and said, "Well, what are we going to call him?" They were all acting as if I wasn't present as they went over names for me.

Finally Luca said, "Let's call him, Street, because he is brave enough to cross that street."

"Wait!" I said. "Haven't you guys crossed a street too?"

"No never," they all said. "Are you crazy?"

"You mean to tell me that none of you have ever crossed a street?"

"Sorry, we always stay on this side. We're too afraid to even go near it," Dots stated as Gray and Luca stared off into space afraid to meet my eyes.

All I could say was, "I can't believe this!"

Finally Dots said, "Look you are here now, and we want to show you around. Please don't be angry with us. Hey, I know. Since you are the bravest of all of us, we can call you, Brave. OK?"

How could I stay mad at these guys when they already thought enough about me to give me a name to add to my collection? I knew that Cornelius would say that it was not a name but was another matter of opinion. They thought I was brave, and even though I didn't feel brave, the name did sound good to me.

I enjoyed our first day together. When I thought about crossing the street to get back home, I had a sick feeling of fear in my stomach and the weakness in my legs returned. I had no choice but to cross that street again as the guys

stood there watching. I had to show them that I was my new name. So I did as before, I looked left, then right, and then left again and ran like a wild cat with its tail on fire. Once on my side of the street, I felt relieved, but it did take several minutes for my heart to stop pounding. I decided to go and talk with Cornelius about my new friends and how to overcome my fear of the crossings because I had to continue these new friendships.

We spent days together having so much fun, and I did find joy with my new friends. They talked about their families, sitting on laps, having ears rubbed, and getting special treats. I didn't share much because I had no nice things to share. I just enjoyed listening to their stories. Most days together began the same way with the guys yelling, "Come on, Brave." Since I crossed the street daily, I no longer had a sick feeling in my stomach or weakness in my legs. Cornelius

61

said that confronting my fears daily would soon take them away, but I should always use caution. Good old Cornelius always was saying things so wise and helpful.

We had our daily schedule. I would cross the street running and joining the guys. We continued running all together until we got to the end of the block. First we would check out all the new trash. We looked especially for any left over tuna in cans, spilled milk from smashed cartons, or anything that looked delicious or interesting. Once Gray found something white, sweet, and sticky. Every time he took a bite it would stick to his whiskers. When he tried to remove it with his paws, it would stick to them. When he tried to remove it from his paws, it would stick to his mouth and whiskers again! We couldn't keep from laughing, but it took him all afternoon to clean himself up and nearly spoiled our whole day. Next, we would go to the playground and let the kids chase us all over the place. Dots almost got caught more than once. After that we would go to the back of an apartment building for a drink of water out of a fishpond. A lady in an apron with a broom would always come running out after us. She kept hollering something about leaving the fish alone, but we never saw any fish. We were only interested in a good cool drink. Finally, we walked in single file across the top of the fence that separated the bread store from the meat store. Dots and Luca always knew when it was time to go home because they heard their names in the distance carried on the wind. They always had excitement about returning home to their families after our days out and about. When I said "goodbye" each day to return home, I knew I would not return to a nice lap, rubbing of ears, or to treats. I would return to the sound of Loud Mouth Pink Feet saying, "I see you found your way back home you nuisance."

So it went each day finding joy in moments with friends until that horrible day. It was the day when the simple joys of the friendships were all taken away. How could I have been so careless?

"Life was meant for good friends and great adventures."

Author - unknown

7

There was a time once of...

The Terrible Accident

One morning I woke up, stretched, and yawned just like always. I ate from my dish and drank some water from my bowl just like always. I rubbed up against Loud Mouth Pink Feet as she stood at the stove, and just like always she said, "Get away, Nuisance!" Next, the door was opened, and I went out. As always I spoke to Cornelius who

65

usually said something wise to start my day. He said things like: "Head up. You don't want to miss anything," or "Friends are treasures, so treat them like gold," or "Have fun, but be responsible."

I passed by Officer Chris, who rubbed my ears and said, "Good Morning, Fella" just like always. I went to the edge of the sidewalk to the shouts from across the street from the guys just like always.

What happened next I can't even explain to myself. For some unknown reason, I ran across the street but **not** just like always. I didn't look left, then right, then left again. I just ran like a wild cat with its tail on fire. I was only looking at the faces of my dear friends who had become my family. First, there was the usual excitement and urgency on their faces because they wanted to get started on our daily adventures. Suddenly, their faces began to change, as I was about to reach their side of the street. Time seemed to be going in slow motion, as I watched their faces change from excitement to disbelief and

then to shock. Raised eyebrows replaced happy expressions, and smiles were gone. It was as if I was making a mistake, and they couldn't believe it. Rapidly the faces turned to a look of shock, which I couldn't reason why. Gray's eyes widened, and I could see the total whites of his eyes. Luca's mouth opened to twice its size, but no sound came out of it. Dots turned his head away from me and cowered low to the ground like he wanted to hide from something. Next, I hear the strangest sound like screeching, and then there was nothing but darkness. I slowly started to hear voices from far off places. Some were familiar and others were not. They were saying things like "Oh no!" and "My dear". The strangest thing of all was that I couldn't see, but I could hear words spoken all around me. I hear Cornelius saying, "It will be OK." I heard Officer Chris say, "I'll take him to Dr. Michael." I was wondering who, Dr. Michael, was and why Officer Chris was taking someone there? I started to experience pain for the first time all along my left side, as I was being lifted. In darkness the pain left me, and all went completely silent.

What happened later seemed to be part real and part dream. I heard different voices and words like badly injured, leg, face, surgery, notify owner, and necessary decision. The voice saying most of these words was kind and soothing. I would find out later that it was the voice of the veterinarian, Dr. Michael. He owned the clinic not far from my home, and it was where Officer Chris had taken me. In my darkness I could hear something about removal of leg. In my mind I was screaming, **"NO"**, but no sound came from my mouth. My mouth didn't seem to be working properly anyway. The next few days were a blur filled with sleep, awaking, pain, and followed by sleep again. I couldn't understand where the pain was coming from, but it felt like my entire left side was bandaged. It was better to just sleep and worry about those things another day.

A Cat's Journey Finding Joy

One day I awoke to the weirdest sound, and I got a sick feeling of fear. It sounded like there was a hissing snake in the room, and it was right next to me! My heart was pounding, and the hissing got even louder, as I breathed more rapidly. I held my breath for a moment, and I realized that the hissing stopped. How strange it was that the hissing only happened when I was breathing. Then it hit me that the strange noise was coming from me! Something was seriously wrong with the left side of my nose. It seemed to have no, or very little, air coming out or in. It also seemed that a small section of my upper lip did not meet my lower lip! In those minutes of panic, the door opened, and Dr. Michael came in. I could see him clearly now, and I could see kind eyes and a very pleasant smile. He wasn't as tall as Loud Mouth, and he wore a short white coat over green loose fitting shirt and pants. He had a strange silver and black tubing draped around his neck that he removed. He place one end to my chest and placed the other ends into his ears. The whole time he kept his kind eyes on mine. The panic left me. I immediately wanted to get up to get nearer to him, but he wouldn't let me. He said, "Just be still a little longer, Fella. You need to heal first." It was then that I discovered something I had not noticed before. **MY FRONT LEFT LEG WAS MISSING!** In its place was a large bandage that went around my entire body. How could that have happened? How was it possible? I had so many questions, and I was so afraid. Then the memories came back to me slowly. I had tried to cross the street and without looking! A car must have hit me. How could I have been so careless? I bet Cornelius was very disappointed in me. Everything was more than I could think about in that moment and sadness overtook me. I lay there in my grief, as

71

A Cat's Journey Finding Joy

Dr. Michael left and turned off the light.

Days went by and with each day I grew stronger. Dr. Michael came in each morning and helped me up to my feet to walk around the room. He would always say, "You're looking better today." One day Dr. Michael gently removed my bandage from around my leg area and body. I was shocked to see for the first time not only that my leg was truly gone but also in its place was a long roll of black threads. The threads were holding the opening closed over the area where my leg once was.

Several days later, Dr. Michael removed the ugly black threads. I was worried that it would hurt, but I hardly felt a thing. I could then start to walk on my own to the food dish and water in my small room. I kept thinking about Cornelius and his wisdom. How I wished that he were here to tell me how I could find any joy in my situation. Just when I thought life was getting better with at least the joy of my new friends, I went and did something so stupid! I wondered when I could go back home and see all of my dear friends again.

One day I heard a familiar loud voice. It was Loud Mouth Pink Feet right outside my door speaking with Dr. Michael.

"I am so glad that we finally reached you, and you could come by to see your cat. He will be able to leave in a few more days," said Dr Michael cheerfully. "Oh by the way, what is his name? The officer who brought him in said that he just called him, Fella."

"Well, I never really gave him a name. He's just a mouser you know," she said loudly.

"Oh, I see", said Dr. Michael in a very low voice. " He is a great cat and has learned how to get around very well." Dr. Michael continued, "I want to prepare you for your visit because surgery was necessary to repair his face, and I'm afraid that we could not save his left front leg."

"What?" Her extremely louder than

usual response startled me and made my heart jump.

Dr. Michael began to explain what he had done to save my life. I realized then how fortunate I was to even be alive. Surely Loud Mouth would feel the same way.

They came into the room and Loud Mouth looked at me closely. I will never forget that face. Her mouth dropped open, one corner of her lips curled up, her eyebrows raised up to a full inch, and she said, "Why he's hideous!" Her next sentence was even more of a shock. She screamed, **"Why, I'm not taking THAT home with me! Do with him what you'd like!"**

With that she turned around and stomped out of the room slamming the door behind her. Now, it was Dr. Michael whose mouth dropped open and his eyebrows that were raised, but not at me, but at the back of the slammed door! All I could do was to give a weak cry of distress.

Dr. Michael tried to soothe me with sweet words. Something about staying at the clinic, and all would be OK. My thoughts went back to the only joys I had found, and now they were lost. I would never see wise old Cornelius again. What about Mouse? What about my friends Gray, Dots, and Luca? My careless mistake had ended the only joy I had found since the day of leaving Mother, Brothers, and Sisters. Would I ever find joy again especially now that I looked and sounded so different? Do hideous things ever have or even find joy?

"Every calamity is to be overcome by endurance."

Virgil

Roman Poet (70 B.C.-19 B.C.)

8

There was a time once of…

A Life at the Clinic

So the clinic became my home. I had a wicker basket with a warm cozy blue blanket. The basket sat in the back corner of the clinic's waiting room near a nice window. The staff in the clinic was very kind to me. They always said "Hello" to me in the mornings and "Goodbye" in the evenings when they left for the day. During the rest of

76

the day they were so busy, I hardly ever got noticed. It was a wonderful place. It was a place for treating and helping all types of animals. I knew how fortunate I was. They didn't give up on me and did what ever was needed to save my life. Yes, the clinic was a good place with good people.

A few days after Loud Mouth left, the clinic voted on what to call me. Since I officially became a part of the clinic on a Tuesday, it was agreed to name me, Tuesday. I wondered what Cornelius would say now that added to my collection of names; I had become a day of the week?

I spent most days watching the stream of animals coming and going. Some animals arrived very nervous and scared just to get a shot. Others arrived hurting or injured. What I noticed the most were the persons that came in with their animals. They had faces full of concern, and they said encouraging words as they patted heads and rubbed behind ears. They had calm and assuring voices just like Dr. Michael's voice and definitely not a thunderous voice like, Loud Mouth. I did not see opened mouths, curled lips, or raised eyebrows when families looked at their pets. What I did observe were the stares my way and whispered comments like, "What happened to him?" Questions were always in hushed tones, but I still heard them. The stares at least were not as painful as that of Loud Mouth, but they did make me feel that I was different and difficult to look at.

One day a small boy started to cry and ran to his mother when I entered the room. I watched him peek from around his mother's legs to be sure of what he was seeing. He asked, "What happened to his leg, and why does he sound so funny?"

Those kinds of occurrences happened almost weekly, and I became convinced that

A Cat's Journey Finding Joy

I was truly hideous after all. I decided to back away from the people, who streamed in daily, and nap in my basket. I made sure that the left side of my body was to the wall. In that way, no one could see my hideous face or the empty space where my leg once was.

At night when the staff left, I ran from room to room pretending I was back at home with my friends running from place to place. I got around perfectly now on three legs and jumped on counter tops and from table to table. I was always careful not to disturb any of Dr. Michael's important instruments. I missed my conversations with Mouse and especially with Cornelius too.

Sometimes I would visit the occasional pet that had to stay overnight at the clinic, but most of those times the pets were too ill or sleepy to talk. For a while, I was happy enough finding the joy each day just like Cornelius had taught me, especially when Dr. Michael and the staff arrived each morning and said, "Good morning, Tuesday." In the evening it was awful lonely being all-alone in the clinic. I started to feel sorry for myself a lot and knew that Cornelius would have been disappointed in me, yet again. It became harder to see families each day with their pets. The pets were held and loved. I just knew there was even more holding and loving in their homes everyday and all through the night. *I* wanted a home and loving arms to hold me too! If only I wasn't so hideous maybe I could have a real home too. I convinced myself that I wouldn't be much trouble, and my hissing really wasn't that bad. Was it? Now, Cornelius would tell me to find the joy right where I was in the moment at the clinic. I decided to stop feeling sorry for myself and make the best of my situation. I had food, water, "Good Mornings", and "Goodbyes" each day. Those were things to be thankful for and find the joy in.

I started spending more time in my basket

in what I called "wonderments". Wonderment was the name I gave my thoughts about what it would be like to have more. I tried to imagine what Cornelius would say about such thoughts. First, he would tell me that wonderment was probably not a word, but then he would probably tell me to keep wondering. I could hear him saying something so wise like: Wonderments are good because they can lead to hopes, and hopes can then lead to possibilities. He did tell me once that to overcome my fears of crossing the street, that I should visualize myself doing it over and over in my mind. Of course, I had to ask what visualize meant, and he said to picture the something in your mind like a movie. With mental practice of visualizing the crossing in my mind, I was able to actually cross the street without fear. The hope of crossing the street without fear became possible by seeing myself mentally doing it! Sadly, I became too confident and made a very careless mistake, which I decided not to dwell on anymore. So my wonderments were like dreaming and visualizing while still awake about what it would be like to have a family like my Mother's. It became my hope of the possibilities of being loved and held. Surely there wasn't anything wrong with having my wonderments. What could be wrong with picturing a home of my own in my thoughts and wondering if it would ever happen?

"There are friends, there is family, and then there are friends that become family."

Author - unknown

9

There was a time once of...

Wonderments Coming True

One extraordinary day started out as usual. I heard the key turn in the door of the clinic, and I ran for my morning greeting from Dr. Michael. The clinic staff arrived with their greetings and affectionate pats too. After that people and pets soon started to arrive. For lunch I ate a special meal of some very good leftovers of chicken and dressing (Dr. Michael's wife sure does know how to cook!) I decided to go to my basket for a little nap, but I needed to do my grooming first. I was sitting quietly doing my daily ritual and did not want to draw any attention to myself. I still faced the wall not wanting to listen to the whispers or to notice the faces of those seeing my appearance for the first time.

Two families arrived at the same time; One with a carrier that contained a small frantic whining kitten and the other had a small blonde dog on a leash. It was the small quiet voice that caused me to glance over my shoulder at all the commotion. The small voice was talking to the dog and kept saying, "It's going to be OK, Buddy." Her voice was so sweet, and if *I* was Buddy, I would have been calmed at once. Buddy on the other hand was shaking visibly, and I could hear his teeth chattering together.

"Mom, why does Buddy need a shot?" inquired the little girl sounding worried.

"Because he can't stop itching, and the

shot will help him to feel better," said the child's mother who looked like a larger version of the little girl. The little girl kept talking softly to Buddy until they took him back to the room for his shot.

The mother went in with Buddy and said, "Kim, have a seat over there, and we will be right back. I know you don't like to see needles either."

I told myself, no matter how much I wanted to get closer to the little quiet sweet voice that I should not. I must keep my hideous self turned away and minding my own business which was my morning grooming. First, I went over my right shoulder, then down my right front leg, and I intended to go in between each toe. I was so involved that I didn't hear that the Kim child was right at my basket. I startled and turned. Before I knew it, I was looking directly into the most perfect little being's face that I had ever seen. She had light brown eyes a lot like

Gray's and her hair was brown like one of my many tones.

She reached out her hand and laid it on the top of my head and said, "What's *your* name, Kitty?"

I couldn't take my eyes off of her face, and she couldn't take her eyes off of mine. How strange that moment was. Instead of her mouth dropping open, the corner of one lip turning up, and eyebrows raised up a full inch, she smiled the most beautiful smile that I had ever seen. How could she look at me without turning away like most small beings? Didn't she see that I was hideous? I noticed that her eyes went from my face to my missing leg.

"Did you have a bad accident?" she said as she lifted me from my basket. She sat right there on the floor and held me tightly in her arms. The sound of my breathing through my squished nostril didn't seem to bother her. She started to kiss me all over my hideous face and hugged me so tight that I could hardly breathe through what nose I had left!

Then I hear the voice of Dr. Michael say, "Kim, I see you have met the clinic cat, Tuesday."

Shockingly her first question was not, "What happened to him?"

No, her first response was, "Clinic cat?" Then she asked sounding annoyed at the idea, "Do you mean that he lives here? He stays here all by himself at night? That sounds very sad to me."

"Kim, I'm sure Tuesday is happy to have his home here at the clinic," said the mother, as she apologized for Kim's bluntness.

My thoughts were screaming, **"NO!" "NO!"**

"I'm not **that** happy here!" Then I felt ashamed because I was loved and cared for by the doctor and the staff, but it wasn't the same. I needed to go to a real home at night like everyone else. I wanted to go to a home where I would be a part of a real family like my mother was with

Lucy and William. I hoped for all the things that my mother had spoken about. Cornelius helped me to discover the simple joys wherever I was and in whatever circumstances, but I wanted the greater joys. While all those thoughts were running through my mind, I heard the most amazing words coming from the small quiet voice called, "Kim".

"Dr. Michael, this cat needs a real home and a real name too. Tuesday is only a day and not a name!"

"Kim!" her mother said. The mother began to apologize again and said how sorry she was for Kim's outbursts. She explained that Kim had always spoken what she had on her mind, and they were working on the "social graces" of how to properly speak one's thoughts.

"It's OK," assured Dr. Michael. "She is right. He does need someone to love him all day and all night. We love him here, but all of us already have more pets at home than we should. In my case I have family at home with allergies to cats. He could also use a better name."

"Oh please, Mom can we have him?" Kim pleaded.

Kim's mother looked at Dr. Michael with the look of another apology in her eyes. At that Dr. Michael said that he would miss me, but he knew that I would be happier with Kim. He assured the Mom that it would be fine with him, if they wanted me.

All I could hear was the many "pleases" that came from Kim, and I saw that tears were beginning to well up in her eyes. What? Were those tears for me? At that I looked up at the Mom with the most pitiful expression I could make. At the same time, I made sure to show only my good side. Maybe she hadn't noticed my missing leg or squished nostril. Then Dr.

Michael had to go on and tell her all about it. He explained my accident, and how I had learned to do anything a four-legged cat can do! Again I couldn't believe what I was hearing when she said, "Oh, that doesn't bother us. I can see that Kim already loves him. I just need to talk it over with my husband tonight. We already have quite a group of pets at our house too." She looked down at Kim as she held onto me like I was already hers.

"Kim, let's take Buddy home, and we will see what we can do. Tell Tuesday goodbye, and maybe we will be back tomorrow."

With that Kim gently laid me back in my basket after another kiss to my face.

She continued to look at me as she walked to the door and said, " I hope to see you tomorrow."

After they left Dr. Michael rubbed my

head and said, "Hopefully, tomorrow you will have a new family and a new name."

That night after everyone left, it was finally quiet enough for me to go over everything that had happened that day. I played again and again in my mind every action and every word that was spoken. I kept thinking about how Kim's eyes had stared into mine. She even kissed my hideous face without hesitation! How was it that she could look at me and not turn away? She acted as if I did not look or sound any different from any other cat! She patted the empty space where my leg once was with such gentleness. Even if they did not return tomorrow, the joy of those moments would forever be in my memory. They would give me great joy throughout my remaining days no matter where I was. Finally, sleep came, and in my dreams I was in the arms of Kim.

I ran to the door the next morning when I heard the key turn. When the doctor didn't say anything other than, "Good Morning", I felt yesterday must have been one of my wonderments. I went about my daily routine and then to my basket. The door kept opening and closing with families with their pets, but there was no Kim. I decided to take a nap since I had not slept much the night before.

About the time I started to drift off, I hear a delightful squeal coming at me. Before I could even look up, I was lifted up to kisses and a tight hug. Kim had me and was going towards the door like she was afraid someone would shout, **"STOP THAT GIRL!"** She kept saying that I was going home with her to be part of the family.

She started rattling off so many names I couldn't keep up.

Dr. Michael came over to Kim and rubbed my head and said, "So you will be leaving us. Come for a visit anytime." He then turned to Kim and said, "Miss Kim, I know you didn't like the name we gave Tuesday, so what will you select for him?"

Kim looked straight into my eyes and down my body and said, "He will be, Tiger, because he looks like a beautiful tiger to me."

Did I hear right? Was I just given a name? She said, "Tiger", and I liked it! It was what my own mother had said to describe me. Cornelius would have liked my new name too. It wasn't what I was, what I did, or just **any** matter of opinion. It was a named based on how Kim saw **me**.

To my Kim, I **am** a beautiful tiger and **not** something hideous. She saw beyond my differences and saw something beautiful. In that moment in her arms, I knew I had gotten exactly what my mother had hoped for me. I have a family to love me! I have a name of my very own! Most of all I have **great joy**. Joy has finally found me!

"Weeping may endure for a night but joy comes in the morning."

Bible Psalm 29:6 (30:5)

Acknowledgments

Gail Box Ingram – Friend and author of <u>KOMOREBI Light Shining Through</u> (a book of poems) who gave me encouragement and guidance on self-publishing my book

Charlie Litton – Husband who listened to hours of discussions and decision making at my side

Cheryl Litton – Daughter-in-law and artist who designed the cover, did all illustrations, interior design and formatted my book to ready it for print

Elle Russell – Former student (and all former students) who enjoyed and loved the story and encouraged me to not give up placing it into print

Sandy Smith – My sister who "loves to read anything I write" and talked me through this project

William Walter – Son-in-law, jack of all trades, and writer who proof read and gave suggestions to improve my work

Author

Marietta Litton is a wife, mother, and grandmother. She worked for thirty plus years as a Medical Technologist specializing in Microbiology. In her fifty's, she decided to go back to college and get her teaching certification. After certification, she left the medical field and started teaching at an elementary school. She taught Science and other subjects for 13 years in grades 3 and 4 before retiring. It was through teaching that she realized that students enjoyed stories about animals. Since her children, especially her daughter, had many cherished pets, the story came from the experiences.

She enjoyed teaching subjects but also life lessons through story telling. She told her students that teachers were not only teaching them courses but also preparing them to live in the world outside the classroom. In writing this story, she hopes to tell an interesting tale about a cat, and also hopes kids will give thought to the lessons that he learned on his journey.

CPSIA information can be obtained
at www.ICGtesting.com
Printed in the USA
BVHW061348230921
617399BV00008B/276

9 781087 951492